Roanoke Colony: America's First Mystery

By: Tracey Esplin

PublishAmerica
Baltimore

First printing

ISBN: 1-4137-2485-X
PUBLISHED BY PUBLISHAMERICA, LLLP
www.publishamerica.com
Baltimore

Printed in the United States of America

To all the authors I've read in my lifetime.
They showed me the adventures inside the covers of a book,
and gave me the desire to author my own.

And to my friend Barb, and my husband Bryan,
for their continual support in this venture.

Table of Contents

Chapter One
The Beginning of a Dream

England, Spring 1522-1584

A young boy sat by the sea and watched as the scavenging seagulls flew overhead. Relaxing at the docks had become a daily routine for him. What was really across all that water, Walter wondered. "I'll be an adventurer one day and I'll find out for myself. I wonder if all their stories are true."

The New World had held a fascination for Europe since Christopher Columbus sailed the ocean blue back in fourteen hundred and ninety-two. And Walter Raleigh wanted to get England there. He was older now, and he was going to go across that ocean and see what there was to see. So who was this Walter Raleigh that was spending his time contemplating about the unknown New World?

Walter Raleigh grew up along the seashore, and was no stranger to the docks. He was born around 1522 in Devon, England, and would listen to adventurous stories all day. His father was not a seaman and so did not approve of Walter spending all of his time at the waterfront. He wanted Walter to do something more worthwhile with his time.

Walter would listen to the exciting and tragic stories of the sailors when they came home from their voyages, and he heard many stories about the New World. Walter grew up learning that no white person lived in the New World, and the land looked very different from his own home, where there were houses and markets. He also heard about the people the sailors called the "red men." What did these "red men" look like? Were they really red? He wanted to not only hear about those adventures, but he wanted to live them himself. As Walter grew up his desire became stronger.

Walter Raleigh became an adventurer and an explorer. His father, who was a gentleman, had always said, "Walter you will study hard and become a scholar." He wanted Walter to attend Oxford University, the best schooling offered in England, and study. This simply just didn't interest him.

When Walter was fifteen or sixteen, he left with his mother's cousin, much to his father's disapproval, and fought with the French Protestants in a fight against their Catholic king. He was not going to be a scholar. And after fighting side by side with the French, Walter then went on a sea voyage with his older brother Gilbert. After that he went to Ireland to suppress a revolt going on there. Not until all of those adventures had been completed did he finally return to his England home. Not that Walter did not love his country, he just wanted to see the world. He was always ready for something new and exciting to happen.

After these quests, Walter's dream grew to be even bigger. He now not only wanted to go over and see the New World, but he dreamed of starting a colony over in the New World. By colony, Walter wanted to send English people over to the New World to live and raise families, just like England. England had already claimed some of the land in the New World, but he knew it would take more than just a claim to really make it English. He wanted to send people over there to settle and make England a larger country. But how could he start a colony? That would require people willing to go, ships to take them, and most important…money. That was something that Walter Raleigh did not have. He did not have enough money to start a colony all on his own. How could he buy ships to go all the way across the ocean? How could he pay for a crew of sailors and captains to man the ships? How could he pay for the needed food and supplies to keep everyone alive during the voyage? As Walter started to formulate his plan in his head, he kept getting stuck at the issue of finances. "How ever am I going to afford this venture?" But Walter Raleigh was determined to get his colony started, and begin his dream. He just needed to find someone who could help him finance, or pay, for the voyage.

Walter Raleigh decided to ask the Queen of England to help pay for the voyage. The now grown up Raleigh, and Queen Elizabeth were well acquainted. Raleigh was a favorite among her royal court, even though he had not always been. She now considered him a trusted friend.

There is a story, whether true or not, I dare not say, but it fits with Walter Raleigh's daring personality and something that he would do. One day when the Queen was out she ran into a mud puddle in the middle of the road where she was walking. Raleigh ran to drop his most expensive cloak on the mud puddle, so that she could cross it with still dry shoes, and not have to go around it. This gesture quickly caught Queen Elizabeth's fancy and attention. Walter Raleigh promptly became a favorite among her court.

So, in 1584, ninety-two years after Columbus had discovered the New World, and many years after Walter had been a small lad, he went to ask the Queen for her financial support. Raleigh talked with the Queen and told her how valuable new land and new materials, like gold, would be to England. If she wanted to conquer Spain and become a world power she would need this new unexplored land and the resources it would provide. Having a colony in the New World would increase England's power and reputation greatly. Queen Elizabeth I refused to spend all of that money paying for Englanders to go overseas and live in an unexplored place where their success could not be guaranteed, but did say that he could send explorers to go look for a possible place to start a colony. She would allow this, and even help with it, on the condition that Raleigh himself did not go. England was about to go to war with Spain, and she said Raleigh was too important. She needed him in England.

Raleigh was so excited! He didn't care that he was not allowed to go himself. He was seeing the beginnings of his dream! He started planning immediately for his first group of explorers to go to the New World. He wished he could go with them, but on April 27, 1584, Raleigh watched as two ships left from the Plymouth, England harbor, bound for the New World. Imagine his thrill as he watched his dream sail to Columbus's New World! "I wonder what stories they'll have to come back and tell," he thought to himself.

Raleigh had heard how attractive the land was and that the Spanish were already exploring and settling. It was warm with palm trees, what we now know as Florida. But since Raleigh obviously couldn't send explorers to land that Spain had claimed, he sent them to the next best place. He told them to go a little further up the coastline, because surely it would be just as pretty there.

Raleigh had picked two captains for his ships. One was Arthur Barlowe, who had served with him in Ireland, and the other was Philip Amados. Raleigh told both captains to explore the coast of the New World, trade with the Indians, or "red men" and to try to build a relationship with them. As well as to locate a satisfactory place for an English settlement. He also had a Spanish navigator, Simon Fernando, go with them. Fernando had sailed previously to the New World, and would be a great help to them.

Once the explorers reached land it was July, sixty-nine long days at sea, and they could barely wait to get ashore. "Land ahoy!" some sailor undoubtedly called from the bow of a ship. I imagine the sailors were probably jumping over the sides of the boat and swimming through the shallow water to get to the sandy beach ahead of them! None of the men, except Fernando, had ever been to the New World before, and they were seeing everything for the first time. Imagine what was going on in their heads! Were they excited? Were they scared? Think about how you feel the first time you see something new. They were probably feeling both a little excited and scared. But most of all, they were glad to get off those cramped ships.

Arthur Barlowe happily welcomed the sight of land and said, "There are good woods full of deer, rabbits, hares, and fowls…the highest and reddest cedar trees in the world." He was very impressed with everything he spotted.

The men spent the next couple days exploring the unfamiliar area. They had landed in present day North Carolina, where it is very sandy, with huge sand dunes, and not a lot of trees. But in July, it was very warm, and it didn't take long for them to run into the local inhabitants. Actually, it only took two days. By local inhabitants, they were not the deer, raccoons, or birds. Though they most definitely ran into those local inhabitants as well, as Barlowe stated. But these inhabitants were the local Indians. The red men as they were commonly called. The explorers were probably feeling those same two feelings again, being both excited and scared at the same time. They had expected to see Indians, and were even told by Raleigh before they left to meet, trade, and learn about the Indians. But they did not know how the Indians were going to treat them. Would they be kind to them, or would they attack them?

The men watched as three Indians rowed their small boat to the sandy shore the men were standing on. Two of the Indians stayed in the boat, as the third Indian came ashore, and walked fearlessly towards the men. He held his head high and looked everyone straight in the eye. But there was nothing to fear. The Indian tried speaking to the men, but his language was so unfamiliar that they could not understand anything he was saying. But to show their good intentions, the men invited the Indian aboard one of the ships, and presented him with a hat and a shirt. The Indian took the gifts and returned, wordlessly, to his boat, and left with the other two Indians. The English men were not quite sure what to think of the exchange.

But the following day even more Indians showed up. Boat loads of Indians came ashore, including the Indian who had come the day prior. Since they obviously could not speak to one another, the Indians showed broad smiles to let the men know they were welcome. They brought skins and furs to trade for more trinkets. The Indians had never seen pots or pans before. So the men traded and in turn, gave the Indians more gifts. The Indians were very friendly towards them, and two of them even helped show the explorers around.

Manteo, a Croatoan Indian, who lived on a nearby island named Croatoan Island, spent the next few days showing the explorers around the surrounding land. The explorers learned that there was a lot of water and sand located in the area. And the land was pretty flat. They did not see any huge mountains or large waterfalls, just the ocean and pretty green trees. The interior of the land, away from the sand and ocean, was very rich, with a deep soil and strong trees.

Manteo even took the explorers to Croatoan Island to introduce the men to his own tribe. He must have trusted and liked the explorers to take them to his home! The explorers quickly learned that Manteo was a friend, and would help them any way he could. He was not mad at them for being there. If anything, he appeared curious.

Another Indian who showed the explorers around was named Wanchese. He was part of a tribe named the Roanokes. They, like the Croatoans, lived on the island called Roanoke Island. When Wanchese showed the explorers Roanoke Island, the explorers liked this island, and decided that it would be a good place to start a colony. The Roanoke Indians were also kind to them, just like the Croatoans. They showed them how to plant maize, which is corn, and catch fish. The explorers knew that the generosity and knowledge of these Indians would help the colonists when they came back to build their homes. The Indians could teach the colonists how to survive in the foreign land. The explorers spent two months in the New World before they decided it was time to start back for England. But did they have stories to tell Raleigh!

When they left to go back to England, they took more with them than they originally came with. Besides the corn and potatoes, which people in England had never seen before, the men also were delighted when Manteo and Wanchese decided to join them for the trip back to England.

Chapter 2
The Return Home

England, Fall 1584 – April, 1585

When the two ships finally reached England, Raleigh and Queen Elizabeth I were both so excited to see them! They had been gone about seven months. That's almost a year, and a long time to wait for word about what happened. And Raleigh and Queen Elizabeth I were even more excited when they learned about the success of the voyage. Queen Elizabeth I was so impressed in fact, that she bestowed a knighthood on Raleigh. Therefore, he was now known as Sir Walter Raleigh, instead of Walter Raleigh. This was a very important thing to happen to Raleigh. Queen Elizabeth I also claimed the land that had been explored for England, and named it Virginia, in her own honor. Sir Walter Raleigh had convinced her of his dream to start a colony in the New World. She agreed to help him with the money.

It took Raleigh almost one year to plan the next voyage, but on April 9, 1585, seven ships sailed out of Plymouth, England. Again, Raleigh was not part of the group going across the ocean. He was still needed in case England went to war with Spain. But since this voyage consisted of seven ships instead of two, you can guess that more people were going. Of course, Manteo and Wanchese were on one of the ships, going back home to Croatoan and Roanoke Islands. They had been away from home for over a year. Imagine everything they saw in England. All of the houses and markets they witnessed! Imagine the stories they would have to tell their families and fellow tribe members when they finally got home!

Raleigh had made Sir Richard Grenville the leader of the expedition. Grenville was one of Raleigh's cousins. He sent John White, an artist, to go along and draw pictures of what the New World looked like. He sent Thomas Hariot, a scientist and writer, to go along and record what was on the land. Since Raleigh could not go, he was going to try to see what everything looked like as much as possible. And of course, Simon Fernando again went as the navigator. There were one hundred and eight men aboard the seven ships. This expedition was a lot larger then the first one, which consisted of only three explorers, not including the sailors. What would the Indians think of all these men coming to the little island of Roanoke?

Chapter 3
The Second Voyage

The New World, Summer 1585

On June 26, 1585, the ships landed. They said good-bye to Manteo, as he left to go see his family and, undoubtedly, tell them all about his stories of England. He had no contact with his tribe for a year. Undoubtedly he was wondering about their circumstances over the past year. Wanchese left immediately as well, though he was not as friendly in his farewell. In fact, he didn't even say good-bye to anyone. He seemed anxious to get home. He had obviously spent enough time with the Englanders.

Without thinking about this strange farewell, the men immediately started disembarking their cargo, and began building a fort. They were tired of being on the ships, and wanted to sleep on dry land as soon as possible. Although building a fort was not their idea of adventure and entertainment. Many of the men had hoped to find silver and gold. They had not expected to have to build houses, plant seed for food, or do such housework chores as mend their own clothes. But since they had nobody else to rely on for help besides themselves, the men were forced to manage all the work on their own.

They built a fort with tall walls made of cut down trees, and they dug a moat around it. But the fort was too small to put enough houses within it, so they built their houses along the outskirts of the fort. They felt relatively safe with the Indians, so there was no need in putting their houses inside the protection of the fort, right? After several weeks of working, they gave their fort a name. They called it the New Fort of Virginia, and they named their new homes outside of the fort the "cittie of Ralegh." This was the name of their colony.

For months, life went well on Roanoke. The Roanoke Indians helped the men learn how to plant maize, and how to catch fish, just as they had taught the previous explorers. That way they could take care of themselves, and not have to rely on the Indians for everything. The Indians were very smart in trying to teach the men to take care of themselves. What would happen when winter came? The Indians didn't want to feel responsible for helping the one hundred and eight men stay alive during those hard months. But all of this friendliness from the Indians changed when the leader, Sir Richard Grenville, noticed his silver mug was missing.

Now, when was the last time you ever lost anything? Or put something somewhere and you just couldn't remember where you put it? That exact thing happened to me last week with a book. I still have yet to find it. Well, instead of thinking he had misplaced it; Grenville accused the Indians of taking it. He didn't even question any of the one hundred and eight men that were under his command, and perhaps one of the Indians did take it. We'll never know. When the Roanoke Indians told him they had not taken it, he thought they were lying, and he was not going to let them get away with stealing one silver mug. He was going to punish them.

Grenville took some men with him and went out and burned one of the Indian villages. And, of course, he did not find his mug. But he did succeed in making the Indians angry. They had only tried to help the men, and here they were burning down their villages. They had taken their time to teach them how to plant maize and how to catch their own fish. And Grenville had destroyed their homes over one silver mug, which Grenville could not even prove the Indians had taken, in which the Indians said they didn't take. (Remember, Grenville could have easily misplaced it.) But, what was done was done, and the Indians' attitude towards the men changed. They now looked at them as skeptical enemies rather than friends. And in turn, the men thought of the Indians as enemies as well. What friend would burn your house down?

The Indians did not do anything to the men. And Grenville did not go back to apologize for his rash actions. They simply kept clear of each other.

Shortly afterwards, Grenville decided to take the ships and sail back to England for more supplies. He had the fort built, food planted, and the Indians under control. Life was a success in the New World. He left most of the men behind to man the fort, and he left Ralph Lane as Governor. Therefore, Lane would be the new leader of the men while Grenville was gone. But once Grenville had sailed away in August of the same year, life was not the same as it had been before.

The men and the Indians started to fight. The Indians had been sitting and letting their anger build until they could not contain it anymore. When they saw that Grenville was getting more supplies, and intending to stay, they went out and burned the men's crops. But at least they didn't burn down their houses, which could have easily been done since they were unprotected outside of the fort walls. But the men did have to worry about being shot with an arrow whenever they went out hunting or fishing. Indians would be waiting in the trees for them.

At one point some of the men decided to go in search of gold. They were tired of hiding out in the fort. If they were going to have to stay there and be miserable, they had might as well find something worthwhile to do. The men left, with enough supplies to sustain them through their gold digging adventure. But Wanchese and several other Indians quickly made their delightful adventure a horror.

The Indians snuck in at night while the men slept at their camp, and destroyed all of their food supplies. When the men woke in the morning there was nothing to eat, but they didn't turn back to the fort. They kept exploring further, certain that they could hunt food. The men became so hungry! They looked everywhere for food but could find nothing. This went on for several days, with the Indians scattering all of the wildlife. When they were walking down a shallow path through the woods, and came face to face with Wanchese and his fellow Indians, they knew their battle would be hopeless. They had no energy. So instead, they simply turned around, with Wanchese and the other Indians at their heels, and headed back to the fort. Nobody was hurt this day, but the Indians had still won.

The real misfortune happened when the chief of the Roanoke tribe, Wingina, was later killed during a battle with the men. The men decided to attack the Indians in one last attempt, and raided Wingina's village. If there was any Indian you didn't want to kill during a battle, it was the Indian Chief.

Wanchese, the Indian who had helped show the first explorers around the island, and who had gone to England the year prior, became the new chief, and he was no longer a friend to the men, as he had already shown. He was their enemy! Therefore, his tribe was now also their enemy. The mistrust and fighting only got worse.

The men started to worry about surviving. They were afraid they were either going to starve, because all their crops were being burned, or killed when they went out looking for more food. They wanted to go back to England. But they didn't have any ships. Grenville had taken them all when he went back for supplies. The men decided to split up. At least one of the groups might have a chance.

Half of the men went to Croatoan Island, to look for food, shelter and to keep a hopeful eye open for some miracle to appear across the water. The Croatoan Indians didn't bother them while they were there. They still considered the men friends of the Indians. The other half of the men stayed on Roanoke Island, and also continued to scavenge for food and look for sails on the horizon. The two groups kept close contact with each other though, since the islands were only separated by a small space of water.

One day in the spring, after the men had managed to survive their first winter, the men on Roanoke Island saw sails on the horizon. They quickly built a huge fire to beckon the ships to come to land, and to let the men on Croatoan know of their discovery. Could it be Grenville returning with supplies? They didn't care who it was. They just wanted to get off those islands and hopefully go back to England. The New World no longer looked like a land of promise to them. They were starving and they were tired. They wanted to go home to England. And all of this fighting had started over one missing silver mug.

The ships belonged to the Englishman, Sir Francis Drake. He had twenty-three English warships with him. They had not been coming to Roanoke, merely sailing by, but when the men begged him to take them with him Drake agreed to help out anyway. At first, Drake offered to leave supplies and a ship behind, but too many of the men were ready to go back to England. The New World was not everything they had hoped it would be. They were afraid they wouldn't be alive when Grenville finally did show up with supplies.

On June 15, 1586, Drake's ships left, taking all of the men with them. They had abandoned the fort and were going home to England. Imagine how packed they were on the already full ships. Living under the ship decks for a couple months must have been very crowded, damp, and musty, but the men didn't care. They were finally going home. And I'm sure many of the Indians, who had once been their friends, now hoped they had left for good. The Indians undoubtedly watched them from the shore as the many ships sailed away, hoping to never see the white man again, and proud of their victory.

Ironically, which means surprisingly, Grenville reached Roanoke, with all the supplies, about two weeks after the men had abandoned the "cittie of Ralegh." He looked everywhere, but could not find anyone. He did not know what happened to the men, and he did not dare ask the Indians for help. But before Grenville left to sail back to England again, he left fifteen men to guard the fort, with enough supplies to last for two years.

Chapter 4
The Roanoke Colony

England, Fall 1586

Raleigh did not know what to think or do when the men returned with Sir Francis Drake to England. They told him about fighting with the Indians, and about Wanchese. Raleigh was disappointed in the failure of his first attempted colony, but still had his dream of starting a colony. Queen Elizabeth I did not have the money to support another voyage, nor did she like what she had heard. She was still preparing for war with Spain, and needed all of her finances to protect her country. Raleigh's attempts were not benefitting her country. And people were quickly losing faith in the idea of a colony in the New World. Nothing had been found of value to England. No gold or silver had been discovered. Raleigh was still determined to start his colony though. But even though he had been bestowed with knighthood, it did not suddenly make him a wealthy man. He had to be crafty and come up with a new idea. He decided to found the Virginia Company.

The Virginia Company was Raleigh's way of financing his next attempt at a colony. The way it worked was anyone who wanted to be a member of the company would have to pay a portion of the voyage, but those same people would also receive a portion of the wealth found in the New World. These investors who helped pay for the voyage did not have to actually go to the New World, and in actuality, none of them did. They were all men who had status and wealth, and were willing to pay the passage for other adventurers, in hopes of gaining riches out of what they discovered in the New World. Now, remember, the Europeans had first hoped to find gold, silver, and pearls in the New World. But so far they had found nothing. Why would that suddenly change? Still, Raleigh's plan worked, and the money he received from the Virginia Company was enough to pay for another voyage. Nineteen very wealthy men joined the Virginia Company. So Raleigh got to work arranging his third attempt.

Ninety-one men, seventeen women, and nine boys made up this next voyage. Could you imagine being a boy, and sailing across the ocean. All the while, stuck in a ship for a couple months, and going to a new place that not many people had ever seen? I bet some were very excited and bragged about their upcoming adventure to their friends. And I bet some did not want to leave their friends behind.

Raleigh chose John White, the artist from the previous voyage, to be the Governor. It is amazing that John White even agreed to go back, after what had happened during the last voyage. He would be the leader of the colony. Raleigh also gave twelve men the rank of gentleman, which was a respected status, and since nobody in the group of colonists held that status, in only made sense to name some men gentlemen. They were to act as leaders also, and help Governor White. The people who had signed up to go and start the new colony were poorer people, and were hoping for a fresh start in the New World. Each had been promised five hundred acres of land to farm in exchange for going on the venture. The men who signed up to go were mainly craftsmen or builders or farmers.

Three of the men who had been given the status of gentlemen were asked to stay behind, so that they could ensure that needed supplies and materials were always ready to be sent to the colonists. And Simon Fernando was, for the third time, the navigator. Going along were Governor White's daughter, Eleanor, and her husband, Ananias Dare, who was also named one of the twelve gentlemen.

The one hundred and seventeen colonists left Plymouth, England in May on their way to the New World. This was the first group to go that had women and children in it. Raleigh now knew that a settlement could not work with just men. There would need to be women and children to help with the housekeeping and have families to grow.

Because of the new problems with the Indians, Raleigh decided it was no longer safe to start his colony on Roanoke Island, and told Fernando to navigate the colonists further north, to the Chesapeake

Bay. This was land that Raleigh had not sent explorers to yet, but from what he had already heard from the last men who came back with Sir Francis Drake; Roanoke Island did not seem like a smart location to start a colony with women and children.

After the stories they had heard about the Indians from the group of men who had just gotten home with Drake, why did all of these people agree to go to the New World? What did they expect to find when they got there? Why would they leave their homes to go to a far away uninhabited land?

Many of the colonists went in search of riches. They thought they would find gold, silver, and pearls, and in turn secure their futures. They would no longer be poor, but wealthy, and able to have people work for them, instead of having to work for people. Others went for freedom and the five hundred acres of land promised. And still others, like the small boys, just went for the adventure. Eleanor and Ananias Dare went to start a new life with freedom and land.

When the group neared land, they were going to pick up the fifteen men who had been left by Grenville to guard the fort, and go on north to the Chesapeake Bay to find a new place for a colony. But when the ships got to Roanoke in late July, before the colonists had even had a chance to disembark from the ships, Fernando told them that he was leaving them there. He wanted to make it back to England before winter. The colonists were shocked! This was the man Raleigh had already trusted two other times to navigate. Why was he just going to leave them in this hostile area? How could he simply do that? Wasn't he worried about what Raleigh would say when he returned to England? But what could they do? They couldn't force him to show them the way to the Chesapeake Bay. Governor John White, his daughter and son-in-law, and the other one hundred and fourteen colonists got their belongings, and disembarked from the ships. They went on to find the "cittie of Ralegh," and the fifteen men who had been left to guard it. It was a short walk to the hidden fort, since the island was only a couple miles long. They reached the area quickly.

The colonists did not find what they expected to find when they reached the fort. In fact, the only thing they found was one skeleton.

The fort and houses were in a disarray, which means they were in poor condition. Governor White looked at the sad state and said, "The place is overgrown with melons, and the houses are burned." It didn't look like the men had been there for quite some time. Undoubtedly many of the colonists thought they had made a big mistake by coming on this voyage. Where were the fifteen men that had been left to guard the fort? What had happened to them? Indeed some of the women cried in fear and dismay and many of the men were wondering how they were going to keep everyone alive and safe. But what could the colonists do with an empty abandoned fort? They did exactly what they had to do.

After the initial shock, the men immediately started repairing the fort and houses, while the women unpacked and helped the men. Since he was the Governor, John White knew he needed to get as much information as possible about the fifteen men and what was awaiting his colonists. He decided to go visit Manteo to try to find out what happened to the fifteen men. He was probably also going to find out what type of relationship he would now have with Manteo, and the Croatoan tribe.

Surprisingly, Manteo was pleased to see Governor White. When he saw him approaching, Manteo rushed forth, and greeted his English friend. He visibly had faith in these new white men. He told Governor White how the Roanoke Indians had killed the fifteen men. He explained what Governor White had already heard. The Wanchese and the Roanoke Indians were now enemies with the colonists, but that he and his tribe would remain their friends. Manteo proved to be such a reliable friend, that he and his tribe later helped these new colonists learn how to fish and hunt wild game, like deer.

When Governor White returned several days later he was very excited to report about Manteo's continued friendship and relay to his colonists his positive hopes for their success and future. But he hadn't expected to find what he came back to. Governor White came back to find one of the colonists, George Howe, killed. George had been crabbing near the fort when he was shot with several arrows. He left behind his son, Georgie, who was now an orphan.

Governor White decided to fight back, but his plan did not work as planned. In the night, Governor White and several men attacked the village of the Roanoke tribe. They killed the Indians that were there, without sustaining any injuries themselves. But Wanchese and the Roanoke Indians had been expecting this, and had abandoned their village. So, who had the colonists killed?

Governor White could not believe their misfortune when he learned that they had killed some of the Croatoan Indians that had been out hunting. They had been using the empty houses as shelter to sleep in during the night. How could their luck have gotten any worse? Surely, since the colonists had now killed some of Manteo's tribal members, he would become their enemy as well. There was no telling what would happen to them with both Indian tribes as their enemies.

Governor White immediately went to Manteo to apologize for his grave mistake. Manteo had known and been friends with some of the Indians that the men had killed. Governor White explained what had happened to George Howe, and how sorry he was for their mistake. He had not meant to harm any of their Croatoan Indian friends. But Manteo and the Croatoans astonished Governor White, and once again showed their kindness and forgiveness, and understood that the killings had been by accident. And to show their friendship, Manteo and his family participated in a ceremony soon after.

Chapter 5
Two Special Events

Roanoke Island, Summer 1587

On August 13, 1587, Manteo and his family were christened, and given a Christian name. Since the Roanoke Indians had just recently moved off the island, Governor White named Manteo the New Lord of Roanoke. Governor White gave Manteo this title out of respect, and to let him know that he was still the leader and the colonists were new to the land.

This was the first religious service in the New World, and the fact that it happened between white men and Indians is miraculous! And often everything comes at one time, right? Well, five days later, another exciting event took place.

Eleanor and Ananias Dare, Governor White's daughter and son-in-law, had a baby. It was a little girl, and they named her Virginia, in honor of the new home they had started. Virginia Dare was the first white baby to be born in the New World in an English colony. When Virginia Dare was only a couple days old she was also christened. Another baby was born a little over a week later. It was a very exciting time indeed!

Chapter 6
The Colony Left Behind

Roanoke Island, Fall 1587

A few days later the colonists decided they needed someone to go back to England to make sure supplies were returned for them. They did not trust Fernando anymore, and they needed to decide something quickly, because Fernando still had not left yet. Though he was preparing to go immediately. He still wanted to reach England by winter. Nobody would volunteer to go alone with Fernando.

It was decided that Governor White should be the one to return to England. He would go to England with Fernando, and immediately return with supplies for the colony. One day while completing their plans, Governor White told the colonists that if something happened while he was away and they had to abandon the fort, "you are to carve into a tree where you have gone, and if you leave in distress, you are to carve a Maltese cross above your message." Everyone was satisfied with this plan of action, and little worried. After all Manteo had just been christened. He was their friend and would help them. And surely Governor White would return within months.

Governor White boarded the ship after kissing his daughter and new granddaughter good-bye, with a promise of a speedy return. He left only ten days after his granddaughter Virginia was born, and that was the last time anyone ever saw the colonists.

When Governor White returned to England three months later on November 5, 1587, he immediately requested supplies, and a ship to return to the colony. If he worked quickly he could be back at Roanoke within four months. As soon as Governor White disembarked from the ship he immediately went to Sir Walter Raleigh for aid. "Raleigh, I have left my daughter and new granddaughter alone, and need to go back with supplies for them as soon as possible." Raleigh immediately started working to gather supplies and ships ready to take Governor White back to the New World. He even had Grenville prepared to lead the trip again.

Raleigh didn't know what to say when his request was denied by his beloved Queen Elizabeth I. England had finally gone to war with Spain, and she could not afford to let one ship leave her fleet. None of Raleigh's flatteries could even persuade her. She needed everything she had to protect her country. After all, the protection of one country was more important than one hundred and seventeen colonists.

However, five months after Governor White had returned to England, in April, 1588, Raleigh was able to persuade Queen Elizabeth I to let Governor White leave, and he set out with two small ships. Governor White left, beaming, counting the days until he would see his daughter and granddaughter. But he was to be sorely disappointed. His poorly chosen crew decided to go pirating instead, and wanted to pirate goods from Spanish ships. After sitting through several unsuccessful pirating attempts by the crew, Governor White watched as they set sail back for England. They had not found any valuables, and were frustrated. They only wanted to go back home. They had no desire to set sail to the New World to look for colonists that were not their concern.

When Governor White returned to England, he only came back to find out that Sir Walter Raleigh had been sent to Ireland to help organize land defenses against the Spanish, should they attack that way. Governor White was alone, and had no means to return to the colonists. Governor White did not make it back to Roanoke until two years later.

Chapter 7
Governor White Goes Back

Roanoke Island, Summer 1590

Governor White finally arrived at Roanoke, with Captain Cooke, in August 1590, aboard a ship named the Hopewell. He had been gone such a long time. It had actually been exactly three years. Imagine what a restless ship trip that would have been, especially since this captain had decided to go pirating in the West Indies for a couple weeks also, instead of going straight to the colony. Without a doubt, Governor White looked everyday from the bow of the ship for an eye sight of familiar land. His granddaughter, Virginia, would have been walking and talking by that time. Governor White couldn't wait to be reunited with his family and friends. But once again Governor White was not prepared for what he found when he reached the fort.

Once Captain Cooke's ship anchored ashore, Governor White immediately started hollering towards the trees, in hopes that someone from the fort would hear him, and come out to greet him. And even though night was falling, he splashed through the salty water, running across the sandy beach, and up to the trees. He quickly realized that in the darkness, and without a friend to come greet him, he would never find his way. He would have to wait until morning. All night the sailors lit a fire, and sang loud familiar songs to comfort the colonists and to let them know they had finally arrived.

As the sun's rays started to rise on the following day, Governor White again ran up the beach and through the trees until he reached the fort a couple minutes later. He was so thrilled, but all that greeted him was silence. The fort was empty. It looked completely abandoned.

Governor White, and some of the sailors walked around in search of anybody. They didn't find one single person. They didn't even find a skeleton, like they had last time. All they found was the fort and the houses in disarray. Governor White did notice that nothing looked like there had been a battle. Nothing was burned. There were no arrows anywhere. And a lot of the colonists belongings, including some of his own that he had left behind, had been carefully packed, and placed in closed chests.

As one sailor was searching, he called over to the others to come see what he had found. Looking down into a shallowly dug ditch, were five broken chests, three of which contained Governor White's own belongings. He found some of his books that he had drawn pictures in and some of the maps he had made. As well as his armor he had left behind. Everything had been carefully packed, and buried under the soil for protection. But something or someone had unearthed the chests and broken them open to rummage through them. It had obviously been quite a while ago, because many of the covers of the books had been destroyed and the metal of his armor had rusted through.

Governor White looked up from the five chests, and looked at the peaceful quiet scene around him. Where was everybody? Where was his daughter, Eleanor? And his new granddaughter, Virginia?

After searching some more, one of the sailors found some carving on a tree. They found CRO carved in the wood. And after looking at the fort more, they also found the word CROATOAN carved into one of the fort posts. But what could it mean? When Governor White thought of "Croatoan" he thought of Manteo and the Croatoan Indians. So, did that mean the colonists had left to go to live with the Croatoans? Or did it mean the Croatoan Indians had turned and had come and attacked the colonists? There was no Maltese cross carved into the wood. Without the cross, Governor White was sure that the colonists had gone to live with the Croatoans. With all of his worry and fret gone, Governor White wanted to go to Croatoan Island immediately, to seek out Manteo and his colonists.

Without delay Governor White and the other sailors went back to the ships, and Captain Cooke got ready to set sail for Croatoan Island, where Manteo and the Croatoans had lived. As they were starting their short trip to the neighboring island a storm blew up, and pushed the ship back out to sea. The ship lost all but one anchor. When the storm was finally gone, several days later, Captain Cook said they had been pushed too far to turn around and go back. But Governor White secretly believed the captain was more worried about his ship than the colonists. Governor White begged and pleaded to turn the ships around and go back to Croatoan Island, but Captain Cooke's mind would not be changed. They were returning to England.

Governor White never made it back to the New World. He never made it to Croatoan Island to see if his colonists were there. He never found out what happened to them. He was left to wonder and worry about his daughter and granddaughter the remainder of his lonely days.

Governor John White did keep trying to find his fellow colonists though. It is not exactly known when or where Governor White died. It was written that his "parts were beyond the sea." That makes it seem likely that he died still searching for his daughter, granddaughter, and fellow colonists who had so bravely and hopefully gone into the New World to start a colony all alone.

After the disappearance of the one hundred and seventeen colonists Sir Walter Raleigh gave up his attempts of starting a colony in the New World of Virginia, but his death was well remembered.

When James I succeeded Raleigh's companion Queen Elizabeth I to the throne of England in 1603, he immediately had a dislike for Raleigh. He did not approve of his constant continued tangles with the Spanish, even though the war was over. He quickly found reason to charge Raleigh with treason and had him thrown in the Tower. Raleigh's knighthood and everything he owned were stripped from him.

When Raleigh was finally released in 1616, he promised King James I not to cause any trouble with the Spanish. Despite his promise, he fought with the Spanish authorities, and when he finally returned to England, he paid for his error with his head.

So, what happened to the colonists? There are three main possibilities that people tend to believe. But since nobody knows for sure, and no definite evidence has ever been uncovered, you'll have to make up your own mind as to what you think happened not that long

Chapter 8
What Happened?

Over the years, and after lots of research, people have come to believe that one of three things may have happened to the colonists. Although everyone is entitled to have his own idea of what happened to them, or where they went.

Some people believe that the Spanish found out about the colony, and came over and killed the colonists. After all, England was at war with Spain, and Spain was trying to hurt them any way possible. The colony was attempted because it was supposed to bring wealth, prosperity, and added land to England. But it seems like a long way to travel, across the ocean, to conquer a group of one hundred and seventeen colonists, when you don't even know for sure where they are located. Raleigh had been very careful about keeping the colony's location as secret as possible, to protect it against any enemies. So, this theory may seem unlikely.

Others believe that the Roanoke Indians killed them. Now, this theory has some more evidence behind it. Remember when Sir Walter Raleigh first tried to start his colony, and Grenville attacked the Roanoke Indians because he thought they had stolen his silver mug. Then, when he left the fifteen men behind to guard the fort. Weren't they all killed by the Roanoke Indians? And when Sir Walter Raleigh sent the one hundred and seventeen colonists over, wasn't George Howe killed with several arrows right before Governor White went back to England? Who's to say the killings stopped after the Governor left?

The Indians could have slowly killed the colonists over the years.

After all, Governor White was away from the colonists for three long years. A lot can happen in that amount of time. Try to think where were you three years ago? They could have also starved the colonists, by destroying their crops, like they did with the first settlers. Those first men abandoned their fort and went back to England with Sir Francis Drake because they had been so scared and hungry. So, instead of letting the Indians kill them, why couldn't the colonists come up with the same idea and leave the area?

The third theory is that the colonists abandoned the fort, for whatever reason, and went to live with the Croatoans. After all, weren't the colonists told to carve a Maltese cross if they left in distress? Governor White wrote in his journal that he was not even distressed when he did not see a Maltese cross carved above the word CROATOAN that was carved in the fort post. Wouldn't that mean the colonists had left to live with the Croatoans? But then, why was the second carving on the tree, the "CRO," only partially finished? What caused the person carving the word to stop in the middle of finishing it? Was he being shot at with an arrow? Did he have to stop carving the word and run for his life? Or, perhaps he simply did not think Governor White would find the word on that tree. So, he stopped carving the word there, and went and finished carving it on the fort post, where Governor White was sure to find it. And why would the colonists take the time to pack up all of their belongings if they were leaving in a hurry, or if they thought they never would be coming back to claim them? Perhaps they had just packed up their belongings previously, to help protect them from weather, and they had nothing to do with the colonists actual end?

We may never know what happened to the lost colonists. Their ending may always be a mystery to us. What happened during those three years when the colonists were stranded on Roanoke Island? Did the Spanish locate them and murder them? Did the Roanoke Islands massacre them? Or did they leave Roanoke Island and go to Croatoan Island to live with the Croatoan's? Who had carved CROATOAN in the fence post? How could one hundred and seventeen people just disappear without a trace, leaving behind one word carved in a fort post: CROATOAN? If we took time to ponder it, the many unanswered questions about the colonists could probably be numberless. What we do know, is we do know that they were there, and that something happened to them. But what that something was, we may always have to wonder. The lost colonists of Roanoke Colony will always remain America's first mystery.